TRICK OR TREAT?

What do Halloween aficionados want when preparing for the spookiest—and arguably most magical—time of the year? I drew inspiration from my own Halloweens gone by. My favorite costume was always a ghost, with its classic simplicity: both last-minute and most concealing in just a couple of easy steps. (My mother is *still* finding flat sheets in the linen closet with ghost eyes cut out in them!) I also remembered things like candy corn and carved pumpkins and great Halloween cookies made by my grandmother's neighbor. These simple ideas are the ones I wanted to revisit and elaborate on to enjoy again and again.

I have my own family now, and we relish the seasons. For us, Halloween starts early: we use a great many craft and decorating "tricks" to spread the spirit around the house. I think you'll enjoy adding the same kinds of creepy details to your own home, whether you draw inspiration from just a few of the sections or pick and choose from all over the book.

I've explored the phases of the moon for "In Stitches," our quilting chapter, and the many clever ways to incorporate black and orange around the home in "Fun House." A trip to the supermarket yielded plenty of inspiration for "Grocery Ghouls," which is simply an updated way to create all kinds of fun creatures beyond the traditional jack-o'-lantern.

And I didn't stop there... I really revel in the "treats" of the season and tried to think of interesting ways to cast a spell over items like cookies, ice cream, and party foods. You'll never look at a chocolate popsicle the same way after seeing the ones staring back at you in "Spine Chillers." You'll be surprised by how bewitching fondant or marzipan can be and how much you will give a hoot about "feathery" cookies and cupcakes at your own Owl-oween Party. What you'll find most enjoyable is the ease and fun of these Halloween projects—and how a simple stop at your local grocery store or discount retailer can yield all the items needed to craft your own inspired Halloween.

So, Trick or Treat? I say hats off to both. And if you see a ghost around 5 feet 7 inches tall lurking about, well, it just might be... you never know...

Happy Halloween!

Matthew

Matthew

MATTHEW MEAD
HALLOWEEN
TRICKS AND TREATS

Time Inc Home Entertainment
Publisher Richard Fraiman
General Manager Steven Sandonato
Executive Director, Marketing Services Carol Pittard
Director, Retail & Special Sales Tom Mifsud
Director, New Product Development Peter Harper
Assistant Director, Brand Marketing Laura Adam
Associate Counsel Helen Wan
Marketing Manager Victoria Alfonso
Senior Brand Manager, TWRS/M Holly Oakes
Assistant Manager, Product Marketing Nina Fleishman
Design & Prepress Manager Anne-Michelle Gallero
Book Production Manager Susan Chodakiewicz

Special thanks Alexandra Bliss, Glenn Buonocore,
Margaret Hess, Suzanne Janso, Dennis Marcel,
Robert Marasco, Brooke Reger, Mary Sarro-Waite,
Ilene Schreider, Adriana Tierno, Alex Voznesenskiy

Published by Time Inc. Home Entertainment

Time Inc.
1271 Avenue of the Americas
New York, New York 10020

ISBN 10: 1-60320-052-5
ISBN 13: 978-1-60320-052-3

Library of Congress Control Number: 2008904768

Printed in the USA

We welcome your comments and suggestions.
Please write to us at:
Halloween Tricks and Treats
Attention: Book Editors
PO Box 11016
Des Moines, IA 50336-1016

If you would like to order any of our hardcover
Collector's Edition books, please call us at
1-800-327-6388 (Monday through Friday,
7:00 a.m.–8:00 p.m or Saturday, 7:00 a.m.–
6:00 p.m. Central Time).

Downtown Bookworks Inc.
President Julie Merberg
Senior Vice President Pam Abrams
Editor Sara Newberry
Instructions Carol Spier
Design Brian Michael Thomas
OUR HERO PRODUCTIONS

Special thanks Patty Brown, Sarah Parvis,
Matthew Isaac, Kevin Thomas

AUTHOR'S ACKNOWLEDGEMENTS
I would like to thank everyone involved in
creating this magical Halloween edition, especially
my wife Jenny and my assistants Lisa Renauld and
Lisa Bisson; Sue Chandler for her baking talents;
Kennetha Marshall for her way with yarn; Terry
Tracewski and her artful hand; Barbara Koppel for
crafting our moon quilt; Diane Bennett for her felted
creations; and Mary and Gordon Welch for all of
their support at a moment's notice. Thank you to our
"kid cast" and their parents: Jill Stoddard and her
children Isabelle, Bret, and Michael; and Samantha
French-Henderson and her children Avery and Dean.
And thanks to everyone at Downtown Bookworks,
especially Pam Abrams and Sara Newberry; and our
amazing designer Brian Michael Thomas. I thank you
all for the tricks and the treats.

Notice: This book is intended as an educational and
informational guide. With any craft project, check
product labels to make sure that the materials you use
are safe and nontoxic. "Nontoxic" is a description given
to any substance that does not give off dangerous fumes
or harmful ingredients (such as chemicals or poisons)
in amounts that could endanger a person's health. The
recipes and instructions in this book are to be followed
exactly as written. No party involved in the production of
this book is responsible for your specific health or allergy
needs that may require medical supervision, or for any
adverse reactions to the recipes contained in this book.
The recipes and instructions in this book are intended to
be performed with adult supervision.

TABLE OF CONTENTS

COUNTDOWN TO Halloween

Anticipation is at least half the fun when you mark the days till All Hallows' Eve with this clever calendar.

Candies, pumpkins, black and orange hues, and nostalgic holiday graphics will get everyone in the mood as you prepare the decorations and goodies for your Halloween festivities. The motifs on this calendar are quick and easy to make and kids will be thrilled not to have to wait for Christmastime's Advent calendar fun. So start your Halloween here, with a preview of the fun to come.

13 DAYS OF TRICKS & TREATS

You can decide if you want to remove favors as you count down the days with this calendar. Look for a vintage **memo board** like the one shown (ours is 14 × 22 inches), or create your own using **spring clips or push pins** from an office supply store. Download the numbered rounds and any other desired motifs from matthewmeadstyle. com or create your own. Add them to the board along with Fondant-Filled Barley Pops (page 8), Candy-Filled Envelope Favors (page 9), faux ferns, rickrack or ribbon, and any other seasonal trinkets that catch your eye.

Hallowe'en

When witches abound
And Ghosts are seen,
Your fate you will learn
On Hallowe'en.

FONDANT-FILLED BARLEY POPS

Colored fondant filling brings out the charming features of old-fashioned **clear lollipops.** Pick up some **yellow fondant** at a cake-decorating store; then simply knead small bits of it between your fingers and press into the lollipop crevices.

To order these pumpkin and ghost lollipops, visit timberlakecandies.com

CHALKBOARD
PUMPKIN

Transform fresh **pumpkins or squash** into quirky decorations by painting with **chalkboard spray paint** and adding a freehand motif or spooky message. Clean and dry the pumpkin before painting; then apply two coats of paint, allowing it to dry after each. Rub the painted pumpkin all over with **chalk** and then wipe with a dry cloth to create a smudged surface. With chalk, draw your chosen image. But don't touch the image—it will smudge.

CANDY-FILLED
envelope Favors

These quick little favors look sweet by the bowlful or at individual table settings and require only seconds to assemble. Download the motifs from matthewmeadstyle.com, then print them and cut out. (Or create your own decorations.) Attach each one with **double-stick tape** to a **small glassine envelope**. Slip **candy corn or other small treats** into the envelope. Fold over the flap. Use a **hole punch** to make a hole through all layers at the top of the envelope; tie a length of **rickrack or narrow ribbon** through the hole to secure the contents.

TreaTs

easy treats

Turn to these simple sweets when company drops by or you're invited to a spooky potluck.

Any get-together will take on Halloween flavor if the refreshments are orange or feature jack-o'-lantern faces. You can purchase holiday fortune cookies at party stores. Buy empty ones and gently insert your own messages with a toothpick. Combine cookies, lollipops, and other ready-made treats with our quick-to-prepare treats to put everyone in the best haunted humor.

orange HOT CHOCOLATE

Get your cocoa into the spirit of the day by making it from white chocolate.

12 ounces premium white chocolate
8   cups milk
1   teaspoon vanilla extract
2   drops orange food color
Whipped cream and chocolate nonpareils, for garnish

1. Coarsely chop the white chocolate and transfer it to a medium-size heatproof bowl. Set aside.

2. Heat milk in a medium saucepan over medium heat until bubbles begin to form at edge of surface, about 4 minutes. Immediately pour milk over chocolate. Stir until chocolate is melted and mixture is smooth.

3. Whisk in vanilla and food color, then continue to whisk until a light foam forms on surface. Pour into 10 mugs and garnish with whipped cream and chocolate nonpareils. Serve immediately.

DONUT hole KABOBS

To make 4 kabobs, you need ¼ cup chocolate chips, 20 donut holes, ½ cup each of blue and orange candy sprinkles, 1 to 2 tablespoons piping gel, and 4 (12-inch) bamboo skewers.

1. Melt the **chocolate chips** and place the melted chocolate in a plastic food storage bag. Snip a tiny piece from 1 corner of the bag and pipe droll faces onto 4 of the **donut holes.** Set aside on wax paper.

2. Place each color of **sprinkles** in a separate dish. With a **small pastry brush,** brush **piping gel** on the remaining donut holes, covering them entirely or in patterns as shown. Roll each donut hole in sprinkles. Set aside on waxed paper for 10 minutes.

3. Thread 5 donut holes onto each **skewer.** If you wish, cut the sharp tip off each skewer with craft scissors before serving the kabobs.

FUNNY faces

There's no carving required for these refreshing not-pumpkin heads, and they remain cute when you cut them up for serving. Use a **black food marker** (found at a cake-decorating store) to draw whimsical or spooky faces on **tangelos, oranges, or tangerines.** That's it.

trick-or-treat
sticks

Tip your favorite caramel candy sticks with orange nonpareils and dress them in Halloween wrappers.

1. Go to matthewmeadstyle.com to download the wrapper pattern; print out as many as you will need.

2. Remove the manufacturer's wrappers from the **candy sticks.** Using a **small pastry brush,** paint the end of each candy stick with **piping gel** and sprinkle **nonpareils** over it (you'll find both at a cake-decorating store).

3. Place a wrapper face down on a work surface. Center a candy stick on the wrapper, fold the wrapper over the top, then fold in the sides. Secure with a little tape. Twist the wrapper bottom around the stick.

scary snack mix

The goblins will get you if you run out of this yummy party mix. Stir together 2 cups each **caramel corn, Reese's® Puffs cereal, waffle pretzels, peanut M&Ms®,** and **mini Nutter Butter® cookies** in a large bowl. You've now got 10 irresistible cups of snack mix. This mix is perfect for filling small treat bags too.

SPIRIT RAISERS

One look at these pumpkin-faced glasses and you'll feel silly. One sip, you'll feel lightheaded.

For the decorated glasses, cut the jack-o'-lantern from **black electrical tape.** (Use the patterns on page 119 or create your own). Press the tape cutouts onto balloon-shape wine glasses or brandy snifters.

For four 12-ounce cocktails, fill a pitcher with **ice.** Add ½ cup **vodka,** ½ cup **orange liqueur** (such as Triple Sec), 1 cup **carrot juice,** and 1 cup **citrus energy drink** (such as SoBe®). Stir to mix. Pour through a strainer into the decorated glasses. Garnish each with an orange slice, if you like.

sweet-n-spooky

Mold marzipan and fondant into decorative holiday eatables

Sweet marzipan and fondant are as easy to work with as kids' clay but better: Sculpt them into small treats, favors, and decorative embellishments you can eat! Rolled fondant is a pliable icing that holds its shape when dry. Marzipan is a moldable paste made from ground almonds and sweeteners. You'll find both, packaged and ready to use, wherever cake-decorating supplies are sold.

FONDANT AND MARZIPAN BASICS

Fondant comes in white and colors; marzipan is almond-colored. Both can be tinted with gel or paste food colors: To begin, knead in a small amount of color; if the tint isn't deep enough, apply a bit more color with a toothpick and knead again.

Both fondant and marzipan are elastic and easy to work. You can shape them with your fingers or roll them out with a rolling pin (a smooth-sided drinking glass works to flatten small amounts), then cut out with shaped cutters or a paring knife. Confectionary tools, which come in sets and are sold with cake-decorating supplies, are handy for contouring shapes, making little cavities to accept beaks, legs, or other small bits you want to attach, or incising decorative patterns on the surface. Use dampened fingertips to model fondant, and if it begins to stiffen, work in a few drops of light corn syrup.

BLACK CROW CINNAMON STIRRER

Make sure your spiced cider will be something to crow over by serving each glass with a cute stirrer like this one. One pound of marzipan will make about six 3-inch crows.

For each crow, tint about 2 ounces **marzipan** black for the body; tint about ½ ounce orange for the legs and eyes. Roll one 2-inch ball of black marzipan, then elongate it, tapering at one end to support the tail. Roll one ¾-inch ball and affix to the other end for the head, shaping as shown. Insert a 6-inch **cinnamon stick** into the "breast" and refine the bird shape as you wish. Shape the beak and tail feathers separately and affix. Roll out some black marzipan for the wings, cut them out, and affix to each side. Shape the orange marzipan into tiny eyes and bent legs and add them to the crow.

SPIDERWEB cake

For breakfast, tea, or dessert, top your favorite sweet bread or loaf cake with a web of black fondant.

For the spiderweb, roll one 2-ounce package of **black fondant** to ⅛-inch thickness. Using a ruler as a guide, cut it into ⅛ × 10-inch strips (you need about 14 strips). Arrange them into a web pattern on the **cake** as shown.

For the glaze (enough for two cakes), sift 3 cups **confectioner's sugar** into a large bowl. Mix in ⅛ cup plus 2 teaspoons **light corn syrup** until combined. Stir in 1 tablespoon **water.** The glaze should be thick but pourable; if it is too thick, stir in more water a few drops at a time. Pour some of the glaze over the web-topped cake; let the cake sit for 1 hour so the glaze hardens.

CHOCO-DIP marzi-TWISTS

These little twists are perfect for nibbling before the real dessert comes to the table. Two 7-ounce packages of marzipan will make six 7-inch sticks.

Tint half the **marzipan** brown and half orange. Divide each color into sixths; shape into logs about ¼ inch thick and 9 inches long. Arrange in pairs, pinch together at one end and twist as shown. Lay on parchment paper to harden for 2 hours. Melt ½ cup **chocolate chips** according to the package directions. Dip each twist in melted chocolate and then sprinkle with **orange nonpareils.** Return to the parchment paper until the chocolate is firm.

scarecrow cinnamon stirrer

Create a stir in your hot cider by serving it with festively trimmed cinnamon sticks. This foolish scarecrow is molded from fondant; see page 20 to make the marzipan crow in the background.

4 ounces each light brown and dark brown rolled fondant (from one 1.1-pound natural colors multi-pack box)

2 ounces (¼ cup) each black and white rolled fondant

Cinnamon sticks (one per stirrer)
Orange paste or gel food color
Natural color string, small piece for each stirrer
Rolling pin or smooth-sided glass
Skewer

1. Roll a golf-ball size piece of light brown fondant into a ball for the head. Insert the cinnamon stick and reshape head as needed.

2. Pinch off two pea-size pieces of white fondant for eyes and flatten with a rolling pin. Flatten two tiny pieces of black fondant for pupils. Affix the pupils to the eyes; affix the eyes to the head. With a skewer or toothpick, incise "stitches" down the middle of the face.

3. Roll out a small amount of black fondant and use the paring knife to cut the nose and mouth from it, then affix to the face.

4. Roll out a small amount of both the light brown and dark brown fondant for hair. Cut into skinny strips and apply to the head, making some shorter bangs across the forehead.

5. Roll out a small amount of dark brown fondant for the hat brim, and cut it out with a 3-inch round cutter or drinking glass. For the hat crown, pinch off a small piece of dark brown fondant and shape it into a solid cone with your fingers. Affix the cone to the center of the brim. With the skewer or toothpick, draw a woven straw pattern all over the hat.

6. Tint a small amount of white fondant orange. Roll it out and cut out a strip for the hatband. Affix the band to the hat. Affix the hat to the top of the head.

7. Tie the string around the cinnamon stick below the head. Set aside to dry for 24 hours before using.

GHOSTLY SNOW GLOBES

Transform a flower aquarium into a spooky "snow" globe with a fondant ghost in the center.

Use **fondant** to mold a conical ghost shape about 4 inches tall and 2 inches across at the base. Pinch off additional fondant to make the wings and affix them to the ghost, dampening both surfaces before pressing together. Add eyes with a **food marker or candy sprinkles.** Press the ghost onto the flower frog on the aquarium base. Let the ghost dry for about 24 hours. Add some small **colored candies** to the glass globe, then invert the ghost on the base over it and gently turn them globe-side up together.

To order flower aquariums (7 inches high, 6 inches in diameter), go to LeeValley.com

GOING BATTY

Glittery fondant bats flocking around a purchased or homemade cake will send a festive shiver across your table. You'll need 12 ounces of black fondant to make 7 bats.

Roll **fondant** out to ¼-inch thickness. Use a 4½-inch **bat-shaped cutter** or draw a pattern based on the photo to cut out the bats. Place them on **parchment paper** and insert a 4-inch **wooden skewer** into the tail of several as shown. Glaze the surface of each with **piping gel;** then sprinkle with **black sanding sugar** (both from a cake-decorating store). Allow to harden for 2 hours; then invert each on the paper to release any loose sugar. Arrange on the cake.

To order a bat-shaped cutter, visit Victor Trading Co. at www.victortradingco.com

marzipan gourds

This miniature harvest is good enough to eat—for dessert! Two 7-ounce packages of marzipan will make the 8 squashes shown, which range in size from ¾ to 2¾ inches.

Use **orange, yellow, and green food colors** to tint the **marzipan** for the gourds; tint a small amount with **brown food color**. Model the gourds, then roll the brown marzipan into a skinny "snake" and cut it into small pieces to make stems. Use a **wooden skewer** to poke a hole for a stem in the top of each squash. Insert the stem, then press the neck of the squash gently around it to enclose.

candy STICK favors

Use your fingers to shape colored marzipan into whimsical witch hats, brooms, and pumpkins—or any other spooky item you wish—then insert a candy stick into the base of each.

One pound of marzipan will make about a dozen favors. Have a rolling pin, paring knife, small round cutter, and confectionary tools at hand. Tint marzipan with gel or paste food colors as needed.

Pumpkin: Shape small amounts of orange marzipan into balls, then use confectionary tools to contour each into a pumpkin shape. With your fingers, roll a tiny piece of brown marzipan into a stem for each and gently press into place.

Witch hat: Shape black marzipan into solid cones, tweaking them to look soft, as shown. For the brims, roll out black marzipan and cut with a small round cutter. Press each cone onto a round brim. Roll out small amounts of orange or light brown marzipan and cut into strips with the paring knife for the bands, braiding them if you like. Roll out a small amount of yellow or orange marzipan and cut out a buckle, star, or moon for each hat, then arrange on the hats as shown. Insert the candy sticks, then crimp the brims as shown.

Broom: Shape a small amount of orange marzipan into a log for the center of the broom. Insert a candy stick in one end, tapering the marzipan over it. With your fingers, roll tiny amounts of orange marzipan into strings for the broom straw and arrange them around the center. Create the binding band from yellow marzipan as for the witch hats.

pumpkin patch tart

Make an easy, super-yummy chocolate tart and dot the top with cute pumpkins cut from fondant. If you're in a hurry, start with a tart from your favorite bakery and just add the cutouts.

1   packaged refrigerated pie crust
5   ounces (5 squares) bittersweet or
    semisweet baking chocolate, finely chopped
1½ cups heavy cream
1   teaspoon vanilla extract
⅛   teaspoon salt
4   ounces (½ cup) white fondant
Brown paste or gel food color
Orange paste or gel food color

1. Heat the oven to 450°F. Fit the pie crust into a 9-inch tart pan with a removable bottom. Liberally prick the inside of the tart shell with a fork and bake as directed on package, until golden. Transfer to a wire rack to cool completely.

2. Place the chocolate in a small bowl. Heat ⅓ cup of the cream in a small saucepan over high heat just to simmering; pour over the chocolate. Whisk until the chocolate is melted and the mixture is blended and smooth. When cool, whisk in the vanilla and salt.

3. Beat the remaining cream in a medium-size bowl with an electric mixer on high speed until stiff peaks form. Add the chocolate mixture and beat on medium low speed until soft peaks form. Cover with plastic wrap and refrigerate until just before serving.

4. To make the pumpkin cutouts, tint 2 tablespoons of the fondant brown, then tint the remaining fondant orange. Roll out the orange fondant and cut into pumpkin shapes with a small cookie cutter. For each pumpkin, shape a small brown stem; dampen your fingertip, touch the end of the stem and the top of the pumpkin, and press the stem into place.

5. Remove the cooled tart shell from the pan and place on a serving plate. Spoon the chocolate mixture into the shell, smoothing to an even layer with the back of a spoon. Arrange the pumpkin cutouts on top as shown and serve right away.

Makes one 9-inch tart

cookie monsters

Lurking in your local grocery store are hordes of packaged cookies that can quickly be turned into the sweetest sinister spooks.

If you're looking for individual and delicious spiders, ghosts, dragons, or even venomous snakes, it takes only minutes to add the needed details to purchased cookies: We enhanced these with a little icing, food markers, fondant cutouts, and nonpareils—and a lot of imagination.

LOST SOULS

Keep a jar of these plaintive chocolate-covered sandwich cookies on hand to cheer up kids.

Melt 6 ounces **white chocolate chips**; transfer to a 1-gallon plastic food-storage bag. Allow the chocolate to settle in one corner; then squeeze the air out and seal the bag. Cut a ⅛-inch piece from the corner (you can cut more later if the hole is too small; if the hole is too large, it will be hard to control the design). Draw a mournful face onto each **cookie**. Work quickly—if the chocolate gets too cool, it will be hard to squeeze. Use a paint marker or dry-transfer letters to write "Lost Souls" on the jar.

DING-A-LING SPIDER

Here is a spider no one will run away from!

80	dark chocolate biscuit sticks (we used Pocky®), plain ends broken off	2	ounces (2 squares) semisweet baking chocolate, melted
10	chocolate-covered cream-filled cakes (we used Ring Dings®)	5	mini marshmallows
		10	pairs candy eyes

1. Dip the broken end of a biscuit stick into melted chocolate and insert it near the top of a cake; repeat to give each spider 8 legs.

2. Cut each mini marshmallow into 4 small triangles for the spider's teeth with a paring knife or small shears. Add teeth and candy eyes as shown, affixing each with a dab of melted chocolate applied with a toothpick.

ICY STARES

Make these quick-as-a-wink—you can even put your kids in charge of this project. Start with **iced oatmeal cookies** (we used Archway® cookies) and draw eyes on them with **food markers,** which can be found in a cake-decorating shop. We used black and yellow markers, but your eyes can be as colorful as you like.

BISCOTTI VIPERS

Melted white and dark chocolate ensures that the serpents adorning these biscotti are totally sweet and venom-free.

Start with 12 purchased **biscotti.** Melt 8 ounces **white baking chocolate;** transfer to a 1-gallon plastic food-storage bag. Snip ⅛ inch from one corner of the bag. Squeeze serpent shape onto the biscotti; let the chocolate harden. Melt 4 ounces **semisweet chocolate** and transfer to a small plastic food-storage bag. Snip ¹⁄₁₆ inch from one corner and pipe a pattern of stripes or dots onto each serpent. Let chocolate harden before serving.

black magic dragon

This fire-breathing monster makes a whimsical centerpiece for a dessert buffet.

24 chocolate cake sandwich cookies (we used Oreo® Cakesters)
½   cup ready-to-use white fondant
Green and orange food colors
2   large candy eyes (buy more candy eyes if you want to make dragon heads only as shown on page 31)

1. Arrange as many cookies as fit in an olive dish as shown (or stack them in pairs to make dragon heads). Cut the remainder in half.

2. Tint about ⅓ cup fondant green and tint the rest orange. Roll out the green fondant to ⅛-inch thickness and cut 3 to 4 "spines" for each half cookie; insert the spines into the half-cookies and arrange as shown.

3. Cut 2 green rounds slightly larger than the candy eyes. Affix the eyes to the green rounds with a dampened finger, then affix the rounds to the dragon head.

4. Roll out the orange fondant and cut a long, skinny, forked tongue; use a toothpick to insert it as shown.

masked scholars

Who doesn't love those chocolate schoolboy biscuits? (We used Le Petit Ecolier® biscuits in dark chocolate and milk chocolate.) Give each schoolboy a mask; his lunch box becomes a treat basket.

To dress him up, mix a batch of **Decorating Icing** (page 118). Use **orange, green, and black gel food color** to tint 1½ cups of the icing orange, 1 tablespoon green, and 1 tablespoon black; leave the rest white. Using decorating bags fitted with #1S tips, pipe the orange and white icings onto the **cookies** as shown. Draw eyes in the mask with a toothpick dipped in the black icing. Draw jack-o'-lantern faces with the black icing; draw pumpkin stems with a toothpick dipped in the green icing.

BLACK CaT COOKIES

These felines sit on cushions made of chocolate-covered marshmallow-topped cookies.

You'll need black cardstock, yellow acrylic paint, a few tubes of piping gel, chocolate-covered marshmallow-topped cookies (such as Mallomars or Whippets™), toothpicks, and black and orange nonpareils.

Copy or scan and print the cat template on page 119. For each cat, trace the template onto **cardstock** and use a craft knife to cut it out. Paint the eyes and nose on one side. Tape a **toothpick** to the back, leaving 1 inch extending below the bottom of the cardstock. Spread the top of a **cookie** with **piping gel** and sprinkle with **nonpareils**. Gently push the cat cutout into the cookie.

SPINE CHILLERS

These cool confections will freeze the blood and please the palate.

If you need a (short) break from Halloween candy, ice cream is the perfect sweet substitute! Add toppings, cookies, and pumpkin faces—or even flapping paper bat wings—for treats that will chill and thrill.

candy corn freeze

White, orange, and yellow stripes are one of the unofficial symbols of Halloween. This candy corn–inspired ice cream parfait is the perfect ending to any autumn party.

1   quart orange sherbet
1   half-gallon vanilla ice cream
3   disposable decorating bags
9   clear 10-ounce glasses
Yellow paste or gel food color
Orange nonpareils, for garnish

1. Let the sherbet and ice cream sit at room temperature until softened, about 15 minutes. Transfer the sherbet to a decorating bag. Transfer 4 cups of the ice cream to another decorating bag. Place them in the freezer.

2. Adding a few drops at a time, mix some yellow food color into the remaining ice cream. Transfer the yellow ice cream to the third decorating bag. Pipe some yellow ice cream into the bottom third of each glass. Put the glasses in the freezer.

3. Remove the decorating bag with sherbet from the freezer to soften. When it is soft enough to pipe, remove the glasses from the freezer and pipe an even layer of sherbet into each. Return the glasses to the freezer.

4. Remove the decorating bag with the white ice cream from the freezer to soften and pipe it into each glass. Return the glasses to the freezer. Remove them about 15 minutes before serving. Just before serving, sprinkle each parfait with nonpareils.

Makes 9 servings

jack-o'-sherbet

Let devouring this smiley pumpkin-face treat be a group activity or present it with a flourish and then spoon it into individual bowls.

Start with 1 quart of **orange sherbet** in a transparent tub. Remove the lid. Draw a jack-o'-lantern face onto the top with **quick-to-freeze chocolate topping** (we used Magic Shell®). If you're making more than one, a bat or witch's face design would be fun too. Serve with classic wooden ice cream spoons.

october parfait

This deliciously colorful dessert can be assembled just before you're ready to serve it.

For 4 parfaits, you'll need 1 quart of **dark chocolate ice cream**, 1 pint of **orange sherbet**, 1 (8-ounce) container of **nondairy whipped topping**, about 1 cup **chocolate cookie crumbs** (we crushed 20 chocolate wafer cookies to make about 1 cup of crumbs), and ¼ cup **shelled peanuts.** Place a scoop of ice cream in the bottom of each parfait glass; add a scoop of sherbet. Sprinkle on 2 tablespoons cookie crumbs. Add a small scoop of ice cream and then ⅓ cup whipped topping. Top with 1 tablespoon cookie crumbs and a tablespoon of peanuts. Yum!

screamwiches

These are almost too cute to eat, but don't delay—they'll melt if left on display.

Make a batch of **Decorating Icing** (page 118); use gel or paste food color to tint half of it orange. Put each color in a decorating bag fitted with a #1 or #2 tip. Pipe designs on the tops of 12 **chocolate wafer cookies** (we used Famous® Chocolate Wafers); let them dry completely. Let 1 quart of **orange sherbet** soften slightly, then sandwich scoops between pairs of cookies, placing the decorated ones on top. Freeze in a single layer on a baking sheet until serving.

BaTTY BomBe

Here's a way to end your party with a memorable flap. You'll need a dome-shape ice cream cake with dark chocolate frosting, a bag of small candies (such as Skittles® Chocolate Mix), and 2 large candy eyes, one 8½ × 11-inch piece each black and orange cardstock, 2 wooden skewers, and double-stick tape.

Copy or scan and print the bat wing pattern on page 120 (or create your own bat wings). Cut 2 small black wings, 2 large black wings, and 2 large orange wings from the cardstock. Layer and tape them together as shown in the photo. Also cut a skinny orange triangle about 1½ inches long to be the bat's tongue. Cut the skewers to 6 inches long. Place the **cake** on a plate. Gently press the **candy eyes** and the tongue into the frosting as shown. Bend the bat wings, angle each against the cake and support them from underneath with a skewer (pointed end inserted into the cake). Scatter the **candies** around the base.

FreaKY FUDGe POPS

If you've never made eye contact with an ice cream bar, now's your chance.

Line a baking sheet or shallow pan with parchment paper (make sure it will fit in your freezer first). Unwrap **chocolate fudge ice cream bars** and arrange them on the baking sheet. Let sit until slightly softened, 3 to 5 minutes. Lightly press one or more pairs of **candy eyes** onto each bar. Sprinkle with **orange and yellow nonpareils**. Place in the freezer until ready to serve.

SILLY CHILLY STICKS

Candy-coated ice cream bars are even more fun to eat when embellished with funny Halloween figures. (Use a variety of bars, if you like; we used M&M® Ice Cream Treats and Dove® Ice Cream Bars.) Affix a **candy decoration** to each **ice cream bar** with a dot of **ready-made icing or melted chocolate.** Freeze until serving.

To order the decorations shown, call Chandler's Cake and Candy (603) 223-0393.

OWL-OWEEN PARTY

You'll appreciate the easy preparations for this fun fall party. Make our owl cookies and a fantastic "feathered" cake, and serve drinks in owl-faced bottles. For decorations, we've created owl graphics reminiscent of the 1970s. You can download the patterns from matthewmeadstyle.com or create your own owl-inspired motifs. For the invitations (left), download the pattern and print out copies on 4½ x 6-inch card stock. Write the details for your party on the other side.

SODA POP OWLS

Juice, soda, or punch... it's more fun to drink just about anything from a decorated bottle. (We used Izze® sparkling juice bottles, because the bottle caps have cute asterisks that look like twinkling eyes, but you can paint any cap or make the eyes from **polymer clay** such as Fimo® or Sculpey®.) If you use bottle caps, plan ahead—you need 2 for every owl bottle. One 2-ounce block of clay will make 6 beaks or 12 eyes.

Soak the **empty bottles** in warm soapy water to remove the labels. Meanwhile, roll out the **clay** to about ¼ inch thick. Referring to the photo, use a paring knife to cut a diamond shape about 2¼ inches long and ⅞ inch wide for each beak. (If making eyes, cut them out with a small canapé cutter and paint them with acrylic paint.) Bake the clay according to package directions. Attach the beaks and eyes to the bottles with **hot glue.** Using a funnel, fill the decorated bottles with **juice, punch, or fruit-flavored soda.** Serve with **bendy straws!**

OWL GARLAND

Add style and focus to your party spot by stringing these fun paper owls across a window or on the wall above your buffet. Download the owl motifs from matthewmeadstyle.com and print on **white cardstock,** sizing as you wish (ours are 5¼ and 6 inches tall). Print and cut out as many as you like. With a **hole punch,** make a hole at the top of each owl. Thread them onto a long piece of **ribbon or string,** tying it at each hole as shown to keep the owls spaced at whatever interval looks good for the size you've made.

IT'S a HOOT!

Our owl-inspired recipes and crafts will set you on your way to throwing a hoot of a Halloween party. Collect trinkets and table décor (such as glasses, plates, and eggcups) all year long to add to the atmosphere. Kids will love attending this bash —and helping to prepare for it too!

HOOT COOKIES

These wise owl cookies taste so good, they're likely to fly off the table. Owl cookie cutters are available at baking-supply stores.

2 cups unsalted butter, softened
2 cups sugar
4 large eggs, beaten
¼ cup milk
2 teaspoons vanilla extract
4 cups all-purpose flour
½ teaspoon baking powder
1 recipe Decorating Icing (page 118)
Lime green paste or gel food color
Leaf green paste or gel food color
Orange paste or gel food color

Lemon yellow paste or gel food color
Golden yellow paste or gel food color
Piping gel
Green sanding sugar
Orange sanding sugar
Yellow sanding sugar
Decorating bags with couplers
#2, #3, and #5 round tips (one
   tip for each icing color)
Small pastry brush

1. Heat the oven to 350°F. Cream the butter and sugar in a large bowl. Beat in the eggs, then the milk and vanilla. Mix the flour and baking powder in a medium-size bowl; then beat into the butter mixture until blended and smooth. Roll the dough on a lightly floured surface to ¼-inch thickness. Cut out the owl cookies and arrange on ungreased baking sheets. Bake for 8 minutes, until just golden. Transfer to wire racks to cool completely.

2. Divide the Decorating Icing into 2 small bowls. Dilute the icing in 1 bowl with water until it has the consistency of thin sauce. Divide the thinned icing into 3 small bowls. Divide the undiluted icing into 3 small bowls. Tint 1 bowl of each consistency light green (a blend of lime green and leaf green food colors). Tint 1 bowl of each consistency orange, and 1 bowl of each consistency soft yellow (a blend of lemon yellow and golden yellow food colors).

3. Transfer the undiluted icings to the decorating bags. Fit a #3 tip onto a bag with thicker icing in whichever color you wish to use first. Hold the bag at an angle with the tip against the cookie and outline the perimeter. Then, using a teaspoon, flood the surface of the cookie with the same color thinned icing. Repeat with the other cookies and icings. Let the cookies dry for 1 hour.

4. Referring to the photos, add other details to the cookies with the undiluted icing. Use the #5 tips for thicker lines such as the brows and eyes, and the #2 tips for thinner details. Paint the foreheads with piping gel and sprinkle with sanding sugar; let set, then gently invert to release any excess sugar.

Makes about 2 dozen 7-inch cookies

To order the owl cutter used here, visit Victor Trading Co., www.victortradingco.com

wise OWL cake

*Whooo dares to eat this charmer? Everyone at your table! It's fun
to assemble from cupcakes, donuts, and oodles of frosting.*

30 unfrosted cupcakes, store-bought or made from
    your favorite recipe
1   recipe Easy Icing (page 118)
1   tube ready-made vanilla decorating frosting
    (to fill donut holes)
2   chocolate-glazed jimmy-topped donuts
2   black jellybeans

Orange gel food color
Red gel food color
Brown gel food color
Decorating bags with couplers
#199 fine cut tip, #2 and #5 round tips
Offset spatula

To decorate the cake

1. Arrange the cupcakes in a single layer to fill a large round plate (ours is 16 inches in diameter).

2. Spoon ¾ cup Easy Icing into a small bowl. Tint with 23 drops orange food color and 10 drops red food color, mixing until blended, for the beak. Spoon ¼ cup frosting into a second bowl and tint with brown food color, for the accents. Tint the remaining 3 cups frosting with 30 drops of orange food color, 9 drops of red food color, and 6 drops of brown food color.

3. Fit a decorating bag with the #199 tip. Fill the bag with orange icing. Cover the top of the assembled cupcakes with "feather" peaks as shown. For each peak, hold the bag straight up with the tip against the cake; squeeze the bag, keeping the tip in the icing until the peak forms; stop the pressure and reposition the tip for the next peak. Work from the center out, rotating the plate; refill the bag as needed.

4. Place the donut tops on the frosted cake for eyes, as shown. Pipe vanilla decorating frosting into the center of each and top with a jellybean. For the beak, use a spoon to place 3 dollops of frosting on the cake: start with a largish dollop near the eyes, then add 2 dollops below it, each smaller than the previous. Run the spatula under hot water until heated, dry thoroughly, and use to contour the beak as shown.

5. Fit the other decorating bag with the #5 round tip. Fill the bag with the brown icing. Hold the bag at an angle and pipe the brow outline onto the cake as shown. Change the tip to the #2 round tip and pipe on the squiggle details.

mummy cooked

No, not a British mom—this party features souls preserved from the past, served up for your squeamish delight.

Celebrate big time with a theme party of rare sophistication and well-made delicacies. The mummy sets the tone for entrée and décor, while a poisonous shade of green provides an appropriate accent color for the table or buffet settings. Eerie eyes, frozen in timeless stares, peek out where least expected. Monster pizzas delight the guest who is too refined or too young to savor gruesome broccoli puree or ghostly meatloaf. Everyone will glory in the finale—what could be more fitting than death-by-chocolate cakes?

menu

YUMMY MUMMY MEATLOAF

MONSTER PIZZAS

GREEN GRUEL WITH EYEBALLS

BLEARY-EYED POTATOES

WITCH'S BREW

BLEEDING BERRY PIE

DEATH-BY-CHOCOLATE CAKES

mummy vases

Put one of these mummified heads next to each plate so every guest has a dinner date.

Start with an assortment of footed vases and a few yards of white muslin; you'll also need tape, hot glue, and black buttons (2 for each vase plus one for a mouth if you like).

For each vase, snip and then tear ½ yard **muslin** crosswise into ½-inch-wide strips. Tape the end of one strip to the vase, then wrap around, crisscrossing as you go; tape the other end to secure. Repeat to cover most of the vase, reserving two or three strips. Use hot glue to affix two **black buttons** in place for eyes, plus one for a mouth if you like. Cut one of the muslin strips into shorter pieces and tape across the top and bottom of the buttons. Wrap the remaining strips around the vase a few more times, taping as before.

TOOTHY GRIN PLATE

Who would expect the plates to be screaming for their dinner? Set the table with these gaping maws; when ready to serve your meal, top them with clear glass plates. Copy or scan and print the pattern on page 120 (or create your own from black construction paper); you will needs two sets of teeth for each plate. Affix the teeth to **plain white paper or china plates** with double-stick tape.

SQUEAMISH NAPKIN RINGS

How inviting—a spider web or staring mummy to keep napkins under control. For both, start with some plain **muslin**. For the spiderweb wrap, snip and then tear a 2 × 10-inch strip; wrap around a **rolled napkin** and tape to secure. Add a **spiderweb trinket** affixing with a loop of tape if it is not self-adhesive. For the mummy wrap, snip and then tear two ¼ × 18-inch strips and two ¼ × 10-inch strips. Wrap the two longer strips around the rolled napkin, taping to secure. Use hot glue to attach two **candy eyes** in place. Wrap the shorter strips around, partially covering the eyes; tape to secure.

To order spiderweb decorations, visit blumchen.com

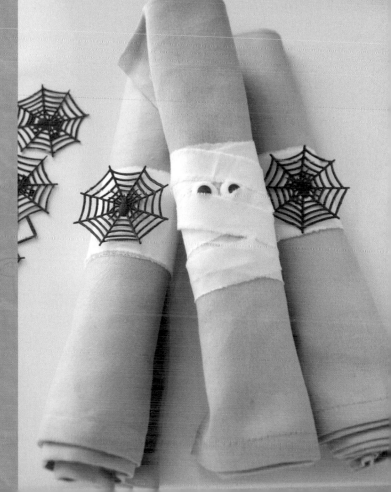

yummy mummy meatloaf

This mournful relic makes a silly entrée that everyone will enjoy.
If you are serving a crowd, make several of these.

Meatloaf:
1½ pounds ground beef
1 egg
1 medium onion, chopped
1 cup milk
1 cup dry bread crumbs
¼ teaspoon salt
⅛ teaspoon ground black pepper
⅓ cup ketchup
2 tablespoons brown sugar
2 tablespoons prepared mustard
8 ounces pappardelle pasta
1 3-ounce mozzarella ball
1 can pitted large black olives

Sauce:
¾ cup ketchup
¾ cup water
¼ cup brown sugar
½ teaspoon prepared mustard

To make the meatloaf:

1. Heat the oven to 350°F. Lightly oil a 10 × 13-inch (or 10-inch round) baking dish. Combine the meat, egg, onion, milk, bread crumbs, salt, and pepper in a large bowl. Shape the mixture into a 10-inch round dome and place it in the prepared pan. Mix the ⅓ cup ketchup, 2 tablespoons brown sugar, and 2 tablespoons prepared mustard in a small bowl until blended. Spread the mixture over the meatloaf. Bake for 1 hour. Transfer the meatloaf to a wire rack and let rest for 20 minutes.

2. Heat a large pot of lightly salted water to boiling. Cook the pappardelle in the boiling water according to the package directions; drain and keep warm while meatloaf rests.

To make the sauce:

3. Combine the ¾ cup ketchup, ¾ cup water, ¼ cup brown sugar, and ½ teaspoon prepared mustard in a small saucepan. Cook over medium heat, stirring, until bubbly and thickened, about 3 minutes. Keep warm until ready to serve.

4. Remove the meatloaf from the pan and place on a serving plate. Cut the mozzarella ball in half. Layer the pasta strands one by one over the meatloaf to look like a mummy's wrappings, adding the mozzarella and 2 olives for eyes as shown. Surround the meatloaf with more olives. Serve with the sauce on the side.

Makes 6 servings

frankenstein PIZZA

Run for your life or munch on this monster? Cut each shape from a **10-inch packaged pizza crust.**
For the guy on the right, top with **pizza sauce,** then scatter **shredded mozzarella** over the chin, neck,
and shoulders. Use **pitted black olives** for eyes, thinly sliced **zucchini** for hair, a **pepperoni** triangle for
a nose, and a larger piece of zucchini for the mouth. For the fellow on the left, top the crust with **pesto,**
make a pepperoni hairdo; then add black olive eyes and a **goat cheese** frown. Bake at 375°F for 12 to
15 minutes, or until the bottom of the crust is browned and the cheese is melted.

*To order the shaped cutters on these pages, go to victortradingco.com
or look for similar ones at a baking-supply store.*

WITCH PIZZA

She looks wicked good! Cut the shape from a **12-inch packaged pizza crust.** Top with pizza sauce. Use **pitted black olives** for the hat and eye; **red and orange pepper slices** for the hatband and buckle, and thinly sliced **zucchini** for the hair. Shape the mouth from a peeled zucchini slice. Lightly sprinkle **shredded mozzarella** over the hat and hair. Bake at 375°F for 12 to 15 minutes, or until the bottom of the crust is browned and the cheese is melted.

GHOST PIZZA

Give your ghost the saddest or scariest expression you can. Cut the shape from a **10-inch packaged pizza crust.** Spread **pizza sauce** around the perimeter. Spread **pesto** over the center and top with **shredded mozzarella** for the face. Ring the face with **cherry tomatoes,** then add **pitted black olive** eyes and a **red pepper** mouth with wicked **orange pepper** teeth. Bake at 375°F for 12 to 15 minutes, or until the bottom of the crust is browned and the cheese is melted.

green gruel WITH eyeballs

People may feel a bit squeamish at first glance, but this broccoli soup is delicious and the eyeball is a harmless hard-cooked egg!

3   tablespoons unsalted butter
2½   pounds broccoli, tops chopped into ½-inch florets; stalks chopped into ½-inch pieces
3   shallots, finely chopped
1   garlic clove, minced
¼   teaspoon salt
⅛   teaspoon ground black pepper
1   cup vegetable or chicken broth
½   pound sharp Cheddar cheese, grated (2 cups)
6   hard-cooked eggs, peeled
6   pitted black olives
Pinch freshly grated nutmeg

1. Melt 1 tablespoon butter in a 12-inch nonstick skillet over medium heat. Add the chopped broccoli stems, shallots, garlic, salt, pepper, and nutmeg; cook, stirring, until the shallots are tender, 3 to 5 minutes.

2. Add the broth, cover, and simmer 20 minutes, until the broccoli stalks are tender and the liquid almost evaporated. Remove from the heat, add the cheese, and toss to combine. Working in batches, transfer to a blender and puree until smooth.

3. Bring a large pot of lightly salted water to a boil. Add the florets and cook for 3 minutes. Drain and rinse under cold running water to stop the cooking.

4. Cut a notch in the side of each egg and press an olive into it. Heat broccoli puree over medium heat until just warmed through, 5 minutes. Stir in the florets and the remaining butter. Spoon the gruel into individual soup bowls and top each with an egg eye; serve immediately.

Makes 6 servings

Bleary-eyed potatoes

Mummy takes a turn for the Southwest with this spooky side dish.

12   medium Yukon Gold potatoes
1   cup prepared guacamole
1   cup sour cream
½   cup mild salsa or taco sauce
24   slices cut from very large pitted black olives

1. Heat the oven to 450°F. Prick the potatoes with a fork and place directly on the rack in the oven. Bake until soft, about 1½ hours. Remove the potatoes and let stand until cool.

2. Cut each potato in half lengthwise. Spread the cut side of each with some guacamole. Top with a dollop of sour cream. Decorate with an olive slice and some salsa.

Makes 4 servings

WITCH'S BREW

This brew has such a wonderfully evil tint you'll want to serve it from a clear glass punch bowl. Be sure the ingredients are chilled before you mix them.

1 bottle (64 ounces) white cranberry juice
1 bottle (2 liters) ginger ale
1 bottle (1 liter) orange-flavored seltzer
Green food color

Mix the cranberry juice, ginger ale, and seltzer in a punch bowl. Tint with 3 to 5 drops food color. Serve immediately.

Makes about 20 cups

BLEEDING BERRY PIE

If you feel the urge to rescue the souls who've drowned here, dig in. We've made this delicious mixed-berry filling from scratch, but if you're haunted by lack of time, purchase a blueberry pie and just add the candy eyes.

2   refrigerated pie crusts (one 15-ounce package)
2   packages (16 ounces each) frozen blueberries
1   package (16 ounces) frozen cherries
1   cup fresh or frozen cranberries
1½ cups sugar
3   tablespoons all-purpose flour
¼   teaspoon salt
¼   cup cold unsalted butter, cut into small pieces
9   pairs candy eyes in assorted sizes (from a cake-decorating store)

1. Heat the oven to 400°F. Fit one pie crust into a 9-inch pie plate.

2. Stir together blueberries, cherries, cranberries, sugar, flour, and salt in a large bowl. Spoon the berry mixture into the crust. Dot with the butter pieces. Top with the second crust; crimp the edges together. With a paring knife, cut 6 slits radiating around the center of the top crust.

3. Bake for 30 to 35 minutes, until the filling has bubbled up through the slits. Transfer to a wire rack to cool completely.

4. Just before serving, dot the top with the candy eyes in pairs as shown.

Makes 8 servings

DEATH-BY-CHOCOLATE CAKES

Give your party a deliciously chilly ending with these small frozen ice-cream cakes.

1   pint chocolate ice cream
6   chocolate sponge cake cups
6   candy mummy decorations
Chocolate Ganache (recipe follows)
Decorating sugar in the color of your choice (we used yellow)

1. Remove the ice cream from the freezer and let soften for 15 minutes. Arrange the sponge cakes on a baking sheet that will fit in your freezer. Spoon some ice cream into the well of each cake, smoothing to level the top. Place in the freezer until the ice cream is firm.

2. Make the Chocolate Ganache. Remove the cakes from the freezer. Drizzle the warm ganache over them; let sit for 10 minutes. Sprinkle with decorating sugar and top with a candy. Serve or return to the freezer until ready to eat.

Chocolate Ganache
8   ounces (8 squares) semisweet or bittersweet chocolate, chopped
½   cup heavy cream
2   tablespoons light corn syrup
1   teaspoon vanilla extract
2   tablespoons softened unsalted butter

1. Place the chocolate in a medium heatproof bowl.

2. In a small saucepan over medium heat, heat the cream just to simmering. Pour the cream over the chocolate; let sit for 2 to 4 minutes. Whisk in corn syrup, vanilla extract, and butter, whisking together until the chocolate is melted and the mixture is smooth.

Chocolate sponge cake cups are available at grocery stores.

To order these mummy candy decorations, call Chandler's Cake and Candy Supplies, (603) 223-0393.

TRICKS

QUICK TRICKS

Fun and spooky decorations set the mood—all that can be created in a jiffy

Here are a handful of simple projects to display year after year and others to set up and then pass out to friends, guests, and would-be tricksters. We supply the ideas and the graphics; you put them together and then just add the candies.

retro graphics wall ornaments

These whimsical wall hangings recall a simpler time. To complete your Halloweenscape, trim a wire tree with small ornaments and trinkets from the holiday department at a craft store.

You'll need beveled glass and scalloped-edge copper foil (from a stained-glass supply store), cardstock, hot glue, and ribbon.

Download the motifs here from matthewmeadstyle. com (or choose your own) and print them out on **cardstock.** For each ornament, cut out motif to fit a **glass piece.** Cut a piece of **copper foil** ½ inch longer than the circumference of the glass. Place the glass on the cardstock and wrap the foil around the glass, tightly folding it over to hold the layers together. Use **hot glue** to attach a **ribbon** loop to the back of each ornament.

For a wire tree like this one, visit handcrafttexas.com (be sure to mention Halloween Tricks and Treats to avoid the normal $50 minimum purchase).

BLACKBIRD wreath

Small beady-eyed blackbirds keep a woeful watch, sure to unnerve anyone who tarries too long near this wreath. Begin with a 10-inch **grapevine wreath;** spray it with **flat black paint.** Arrange **7 faux blackbirds** and **12 faux quail eggs** on the wreath and affix with **hot glue,** tucking a few **black marabou feathers** under them as you do so. Add a few more feathers as you wish.

Copy or scan and print the faces on page 121, then cut them out (medium-weight cardstock works best). Spray a **straw basket** with **flat black paint;** let dry completely. Set the basket on its side. Glue the cutouts to the dry basket with **quick-setting craft glue;** let it dry completely. Spread **decoupage medium** (such as Mod Podge®) over one of the cutouts with a **small paintbrush.** Sprinkle with **orange glitter** (use a blend of oranges for a more fiery glow). Repeat for each remaining cutout. Let the cutouts dry completely before standing the basket upright. Gently remove any loose glitter with a clean paintbrush.

trick or treat tower

A wire basket tree makes a fun decorative accent that dispenses favors too. Fill **small gift boxes** with **sweets** or other treats; wrap them in **black or orange paper,** adding contrasting paper bands cut with **scalloped-blade scissors.** Tie each with **rick-rack, ribbon, or cord,** adding a small trinket if you wish. Fill small **crepe paper favor baskets** with **candies** and hang them from the basket edges.

To order favor baskets, visit blumchen.com

For wire basket trees like this one, visit handcrafttexas.com (be sure to mention Halloween Tricks and Treats *to avoid the normal $50 minimum purchase).*

cast-a-spell mugs

Send a spooky message with **mugs, glasses, or paper cups** embellished with letters. Download the alphabet from matthewmeadstyle.com (or create your own). Affix a single letter to each mug with **double-stick tape or decoupage medium** (such as Mod Podge®). Place a second letter on the opposite side of each mug to provide even more spelling options. Fill with candy and offer as party favors.

TINY TREAT BOXES

These "print-and-fold" packages are as sweet as the candies or other sentimental tokens inside. Download the patterns from matthewmeadstyle.com and print onto **medium-weight orange cardstock.** Following the guides, cut the patterns out. Fold each along the long lines; overlap the long side extensions and secure with **double-stick tape** or craft glue. Tuck in the flaps at one end, fill with **tiny treats,** and close the other end.

FRAMED memorials

Pay homage to the masters of creepy with this eerie entryway decoration. Use ours as inspiration, or choose your own Halloween-inspired words, numbers, or phrases. Write or print them on **tea-colored paper,** using an old-fashioned script or calligraphy font. Place in a purchased **black collage frame** (ours is from Target) or place in individual frames and hang them grouped together.

Grocery Ghouls

If your kids think vegetables are creepy, they're right! Look at all those odd lumps, bumps, and twisty stems (you may see them staring back at you!)

Pumpkin carving is just the beginning of the fun to be had with autumn's bounty of produce. If you can cut a notch with a paring knife, you can put a ghoulish face on fresh produce; harmless eggplants, corn on the cob, or carrots are creepy when they fix you with a sinister stare. Or transform potatoes into crawly spiders and squash into eerie grinning candleholders. The produce department will never look the same!

Arachnophobia

JACK OH! LANTERN

Pumpkins often have the coolest stems. When you shop for a pumpkin to carve, turn it on its side to see what sort of nose the stem will make—surprised, spooky, mean, or funny—then let the stem guide the style of the other features.

1. Turn the pumpkin on its side. With a kitchen knife, cut a hole in the bottom, making it no larger than needed for you to scoop out the insides. If you are able to get it out in one piece, set the cutout aside to use as a plug later.

2. Clean out the pumpkin interior.

3. Using the stem as the nose, draw eyes, a mouth, and any other facial features you wish on the pumpkin.

4. Using a paring knife or carving tool, cut away the outer rind in each eye; leave the golden flesh as shown. Use a paring knife to cut out the mouth. If you've drawn other features, cut them out partially or completely as you wish.

5. Break a toothpick in half. Insert one half in each eye where you want the pupil to be; leave about $3/8$ inch extending. Cut a red grape crosswise in half. Place each half, cut-side down, onto the toothpick halves.

corn-on-the-cob SPIES

Fresh corn with an unflinching black-eyed pea gaze will unnerve your friends. Steam the ears first if you're serving for dinner.

For each cob, peel away half the husk. Choose two kernels for the eye location, then slit each one with a paring knife and insert a **black-eyed pea.** Arrange in a napkin-lined bowl or basket.

GHOULISH Grin candleholders

Unusual or exotic squash and gourds, especially ones with toothless grins like these chayote squash, give you a head start on the character for veggie candleholders.

Once you've found a **squash or gourd** with the right "mouth," carve a spot for a **tea light** with a paring knife or grapefruit spoon. Cut a small cavity for each eye with a paring knife and insert **black-eyed peas, lentils, or other dried legumes** to make bleary eyes.

tapered terrors

Skinny **carrots** with quirky shapes and intense **black-eyed pea** eyes only look like creepy orange candles, and any visitor will be sure to give them a second glance. Wash and peel the carrots first if you think your guests will want to nibble. With a paring knife, cut two little notches where you want the eyes to be and firmly press the peas into them.

SPIDER SPUDS

Make a gang of these for a squirmish event. We used small purple potatoes, but spuds of various shapes and colors will make a truly terrifying infestation.

If you wish, rub the **potato** with **cooking oil** to give it a sheen. Wipe off any excess oil before continuing. With a paring knife, cut two small cavities at one end of each potato where you want the eyes to be; press a **black-eyed pea** into each. For the legs, cut six 3-inch-long pieces of **pussy willow** or other flexible twig. Gently bend a joint into each leg. With a **skewer,** poke three holes along each side of the potato; insert a leg in each.

an eye for eggplant

With their long stems and soft funny caps, Thai eggplants have natural personalities, which you can enhance by adding eyes with a little acrylic paint.

These unusual veggies come from the exotic produce section in a grocery store or specialty food market. Use **small paintbrushes or paint pens** to give each **eggplant** a disconcerting stare. Then tape or tie one end of a length of **thin, stiff cord** (about 8 inches long) to a **foil-wrapped candy,** then tie the other end around the eggplant stem.

SHEEPY HOLLOW

These felted whimsies will add an adorably scary accent to your Halloween décor.

Felting wool is all the rage—if you've never done it, these odd little characters offer the perfect excuse to give it a try. Begin with wool roving (soft, colorful fibers not yet spun into yarn, left), shape it with your fingers, and then poke it repeatedly with a sharp, barbed needle to secure and refine the contours and make the surface smooth (see Needle Felting Basics, page 84). Or start with readymade felt and whip up our candy corn pincushions.

neeDLe FeLTING Basics

You can find roving at a yarn shop, crafts supply store, or online. Needle felting is very easy but not for young children—the needles are very sharp and the felting process requires a quick, firm poking motion with accurate aim. The needles come with several different types of points; different people prefer different ones, so ask your retailer for a suggestion. You'll also need a block of upholstery foam (at least 3 inches thick) to protect your work surface from the needles as you poke them into the felt.

To make a sculpture, tear off a length of roving. Place your hands palm up, with the fingertips touching, and hold the roving under your thumbs; roll the roving under your thumbs to form it into a tight ball or other shape roughly the basic contour of whatever you wish to make—for example, for a pumpkin or head you'd start with a sphere. Then hold it in one hand and jab it repeatedly with the needle to secure the shape; rotate the roving shape so you poke the entire surface.

If the item you are making is large, start with a small center ball, felt it as described above, and then add more roving around it. **To create a slightly indented area,** just poke it more in that area so it depresses. **To create a raised area,** such as cheeks or a nose, roughly form a small bit of roving into the desired shape, place it on the felted base shape, and poke it into position with the needle. **To add a section of another color,** simply lay it on top and poke it into the base, or **for an extension, such as a stem,** sculpt it separately, then hold it against the base where you want to attach it and secure it by poking with the needle. Practice will show you that your imagination is the only limit to this craft.

FeLTeD jacks

Simple jack-o'-lanterns are a fine choice for a first project if you're just learning to make felted wool sculptures. These are about 4 and 6 inches in diameter; make yours as big or small as you like. Be creative with smily or scary features.

grinning arachnid

Spiderphobes may or may not be amused by this guy. Follow the Needle Felting Basics at left and make him 2½ inches high and 3 inches across; add black pipe-cleaner legs and perch him where he ought not to be.

mini-pumpkin centerpiece

Felted wool pumpkins make a charming seasonal centerpiece that never gets moldy and keeps forever. These range from 2½ to 6 inches in diameter; to make them, follow Needle Felting Basics at left, poking extra holes to make the pumpkin ridges.

LAUGHING GHOUL PUMPKIN

Is he a pumpkin, a gremlin, or a naughty sprite who's lost his body? You decide. He's about 6½ inches in diameter. Making him is fun for anyone who has mastered the art of sculpting wool roving; Needle Felting Basics on page 84 will guide you in adding the stem and facial features that give this guy real personality.

GHOST GARLAND

Hang a string of these moaning felt ghosts across a doorway or from your mantel. You'll need white felt, a felting needle, a large piece of upholstery foam, white and black wool roving, a length of loosely twisted black yarn, a sewing needle, and white thread.

Copy or scan and print the ghost patterns on page 122, enlarging as desired (ours are about 7½ inches long). Trace the ghosts onto the felt and cut out. (Or cut your own ghosts freehand.) One at a time, lay the ghosts on the **foam block,** place a small bit of **white roving** at the end of each arm, and poke it into place with the **felting needle.** Use tiny bits of **black roving** to make the eyes and nose, poking each into place with the felting needle. Attach the ghosts to the **black yarn** and with white thread.

The little black and white balls add interest between each ghost. Make them any size you like (ours are about 1 inch in diameter).

candy corn pincushion

*These small felt pincushions will be appreciated by anyone who sews or wants a
festive way to display jewelry or pins.*

2   6 × 5-inch pieces each white and brown felt
1   6 × 5-inch piece orange felt
Quick-setting craft glue
White thread
Polyester stuffing

Scan or copy the patterns on page 123 and print them out. For each pincushion, cut a whole triangle
from 1 piece of white felt and 1 piece of brown. Use the cut-up pattern to create the stripes: use brown
for the bottom stripe, then create the middle stripe with orange felt. Cut the top strip from white felt.

Spread quick-setting craft glue on the large white triangle. Position the brown stripe over the bottom
section and press into place. Repeat with orange and white stripes, using the photo as your guide.

With the striped side up, lay the white triangle on the large brown triangle. Sew them together along
the edges, leaving a small opening on one side. Fill with stuffing, then sew the edges together to close.

FUN HOUSE

Spookify every room of the house with items you already have.

Mummies, witches, staring eyes, and ghosts make Halloween as spooky as can be. Use old sheets, paper muffin cups, eggs, and marshmallows to create weird and wonderful decorations. Cleverly arranged in creepy vignettes, they're sure to startle!

SIT... IF YOU DARE

Warn everyone of impending frightful festivities with a painted and stenciled chair.

Start with an **unfinished wooden chair.** Measure the area to stencil, then purchase **letter stencils** that will fit. Paint the entire chair with **flat black latex paint** (you'll need about 1 quart for the whole project). Let dry completely, then mask off the edges of the area to be stenciled with **painter's masking tape.** Fill in with **flat white latex paint.** When dry, remove the masking tape. Arrange the stencils on the white background (if they overlap, mark their position and remove the ones that are in the way). Pour a little of the black paint onto a **paper plate.** Dip a **stencil brush** into it, then tap off the excess paint on a **paper towel.** Holding the stencil tightly against the chair, tap the brush onto the open area of the stencil. Repeat until the warning is completely painted; be sure to let each letter dry before covering with another stencil.

magic cottage

Keep little tricksters busy with a **cardboard playhouse** decorated for the season. These fold-together dwellings are easy to find online or in toy stores. Ours is about 4½ feet wide and 4 feet tall. We covered it with **wallpaper remnants** attached with **double-stick carpet tape.** Our courtyard is decorated with pumpkins, a miniature urn, and seasonal trinkets. We found the man-in-the-moon (also shown on page 89) on eBay—a great source for surprising decor.

To order this cardboard playhouse, visit www.coolkidsfurniture.com

90

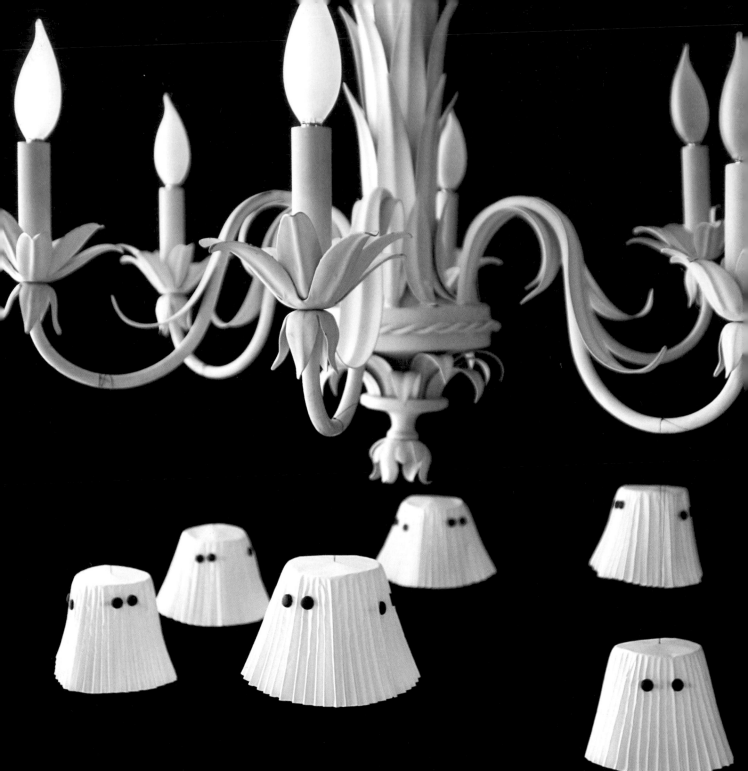

HANGING GHOSTIES

We've always felt there must be another use for pleated paper cupcake cups, and finally we discovered that they make amusing ghostly spirits. Use **jumbo or king-size cupcake liners.** Pierce each one with at least one pair of **black paper-brad** eyes (use two or three pairs to see eyes from more angles). If you can't find black brads at your craft or office-supply store, paint some brass ones with a **black paint marker.**

To hang them, thread a **needle** with **monofilament or black thread,** doubled and knotted, and pierce a paper liner from the inside. Pull the needle through until the liner sits on the knot. Cut the monofilament next to the needle, then tie the ends together to make a hanging loop.

To order king-size cupcake liners, visit wilton.com

mummified heads

Your friends will be spooked by these eerie mummified "severed heads." For each head, assemble a **14- or 18-inch paper lantern** according to the package directions. With scissors, clip into the edge of an **old white sheet** at 2-inch intervals. Tear the sheet into strips (one queen-size sheet yields enough strips to wrap 4 lanterns). Attach one end of a strip to the top of a lantern with **white masking tape,** then wrap the strip repeatedly around the lantern and secure the other end with tape. Repeat with more strips as needed. Copy or scan and print the eye patterns on page 124 and use them to cut out the eyes from **black felt** (or create your own eyes). Affix them to the cloth cover with **craft glue.** Put eyes on the backs of the heads too, if you like.

To order paper lanterns, visit pearlriver.com or call (212) 431-4770

OPTICAL ILLUSION

An offering of edible eyeballs isn't an everyday treat, but this is Halloween and these eyeballs are marshmallows. To be really ghoulish, you can roast them over a fire and watch them weep! Remove **large or mini marshmallows** from their packages. Allow them to air-dry for about 1 hour so their surface hardens slightly. Use a **black food marker** (from a cake-decorating shop) to draw a variety of pupils or eyes on single or paired marshmallows. Tuck the eyeballs onto a **wire tree form,** which you can find in a craft or Christmas store.

For a wire tree similar to this one, visit handcrafttexas.com (be sure to mention Halloween Tricks and Treats *to avoid the normal $50 minimum purchase).*

93

poison

MEASURING INSTRUMENTS

GHOSTIES everlasting

Classic 7-minute frosting doesn't look as sweet when piped into eggcups and embellished with candy eyes.

1½ cups sugar
⅓   cup cold water
2   egg whites
¼   teaspoon cream of tartar or 2 teaspoons light corn syrup
1   teaspoon vanilla extract (omit if not eating)
Plastic food storage bag
Small sugar candy eyes, 2 for each ghost
Eggcups, cordial glasses, or any small dish or bowl

To make the frosting:
1. Combine the sugar, water, egg whites, and cream of tartar in the top of a double boiler. Using an electric mixer on low speed, beat the ingredients for 30 seconds to combine.

2. Boil a small amount of water in the bottom of the double boiler. Add the top part of the double boiler. Cook the frosting on medium heat, beating constantly with the mixer on high, for about 7 minutes or until the frosting forms stiff peaks when the beaters are lifted. Remove the top of the double boiler from the bottom and, if using the vanilla extract, stir it in with a spoon or rubber spatula. Beat the frosting for 2 or 3 minutes more or until it is spreadable. Allow the frosting to cool until it is slightly warm or at room temperature.

To make the ghosties
Spoon the frosting into the plastic food storage bag, then snip off one corner of the bag, creating a ¼-inch opening. Referring to the photo, pipe the frosting into the eggcups one at a time. Applying pressure to the bag, squeeze out enough frosting to fill the cup. Gradually decrease the pressure as you slowly lift the bag until the ghostie is the desired size. Stop the pressure and lift off the bag. Press the candy eyes into position (use tweezers for better control). Once dry, wrap each ghostie in its container in tissue paper and store in a cool, dry place.

Makes 4 cups frosting, enough for about 8 ghosties. The frosting becomes rock hard if left to air-dry for 2 weeks. You can eat them when fresh if you wish or save them for decorations in the future.

eggs in disguise

Here's a funny way to serve soft-boiled or hard-cooked eggs for Halloween breakfast. (Or use blown shells for a nonperishable display.)

To dress the eggs:
Trace the mask and hat patterns on page 124. Cut them out and trace as many egg disguises as desired on **black construction paper.** To make a mask, cut out the pattern, using a **craft knife** for the eyeholes. Poke a hole at each side of the mask with a **needle** and thread a **knotted string** through each hole, then tie the strings together at the back of the egg. To make a hat, form the top into a cone, overlapping and taping as indicated. Cut tabs around the inside of the brim as indicated. Fold up the tabs and **tape or glue** to the inside of the cone.

To display:
We used an old-fashioned egg carrier that we found at a flea market, but you can display these masked eggs however you like: rest the eggs atop large spools of thread or in a gray cardboard egg carton. Or fill a basket with black excelsior (soft shredded wood used as packing material) to make a cozy nest.

WITCH'S COAT RACK

Get prepped to fly off on an adventure: Paint a **hat rack** black
and mount it on your wall. Add some seriously magic **props,**
like an ornate key to the dungeon, wire star, and quaint treat
bucket, along with the essential wardrobe: a striped sash, black
cloak (these are easy to pick up where costumes are sold), our
Posh Witch's Hat (page 101), and knitted **Wicked Witch
Stockings** (right). Rest a **getaway broom** across the hooks
and top everything off with a **bird ornament** and a **"save
the date" notice** made on your computer.

WICKED WITCH STOCKINGS

Everyone knows a witch's toes are as sharply pointed as her nose. Here's how to make socks to fit.

2 skeins (3.5 ounces/220 yards each) white worsted-weight yarn
2 skeins (3.5 ounces/220 yards each) black worsted-weight yarn
size 4 (3.5mm) double-pointed needles
size 6 (4.5mm) double-pointed needles

1. Use a standard worsted-weight sock pattern (24 stitches and 32 rows equal 4 inches/10cm in stockinette stitch on size 6 needles). **Calf:** Using white yarn and size 4 needles, cast on following the directions for the largest size in your sock pattern. Work the ribbing in the round as indicated until the work measures 1½ inches from the beginning; change to size 6 needles and black yarn.

2. Continue to follow the pattern, changing colors every 1 to 1¾ inches to make stripes, until the work measures 21 to 22 inches from the beginning, ending with a complete white stripe.

3. Heel: Change to black and work the heel as indicated in the pattern.

4. Foot: Work as established for 11 inches. Count the stitches, divide in half, place a marker at the beginning of the next round and halfway across it.

5. Toe: Next round: K2tog, work to next marker, K2tog. Next 5 rounds: work even. Continue in this manner to decrease 2 sts every 6th round until 12 sts remain; then decrease every 5th round until 4 sts remain. Cut the yarn and thread it through the 4 sts; pull tight and pass the cut end to the inside. Repeat for the second sock.

wall eyes

Ask your guests to name the creatures who donated
their eyes to this disconcerting display: give an
award for the most imaginative answer. To make
them, assemble **assorted white plates** in pairs.
Then copy or scan and print the eyes on page 125,
resizing as needed.
Attach eyes to plates
with **double-stick
tape.** Or paint eyes
on plates freehand
using **acrylic paint** and
a small **paintbrush.** Hang the
plates with **plate hangers,**
which you can get in any
craft or hardware store.

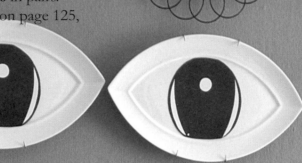

paper BaG Brooms

Any witch who chooses one of these party favors will find a can full of candies tucked inside the bristles. Small candies work best.

Fill 1 empty **coffee can** halfway with candy and place it in a **brown paper lunch bag.** Wrap 6 or 7 thin 14-inch **twigs** together around their middle with 1 yard of twine, tying to secure; wrap again near each end with an additional yard of twine. Insert the twig handle into the candy in the can; then fill the can with additional candy, mounding at the top. Gather the bag around the handle and tie with a 1-foot piece of twine. Cut the bottoms out of 2 brown paper lunch bags, then cut the lower portion of each into strips about 4½ inches deep and ½ inch wide. One at a time, slide the cut-up bags over the first one, gather the top around the handle and tie with a piece of twine. Wrap 1 yard of twine around the "bristles" at the top of the can. Support from the bottom when moving.

POSH WITCH'S HaT

Craft stores and costume shops offer a selection of **witch hats** at Halloween. For a table decoration or to wear, buy one and dress it up with a **purple velvet band** and a **rhinestone buckle.** To make the band, measure the hat around the base of the crown and add several inches for an overlap. Measure the inside height of your buckle. Add 1 inch to each dimension and cut 2 pieces of velvet to this size. Place them right sides together and sew around all edges, leaving an opening for turning. Turn right side out. Slide the buckle onto one end. Place the sash on the hat as shown, and attach with **hot glue or craft glue.**

TICK TOCK, TICK TOCK

The relentless repeat that marks the minutes till the spirits break loose may sound ominous, but the face of this clock is only as haunting as you want it to be. You'll need a **clock** that has windows for photos (from a mass-market department store; ours is made by Karlsson). Disassemble it according to the package directions to insert photos. Coat the face and case with a couple of coats of **orange spray paint** (let paint dry completely between coats).

Using the windows as templates, choose graphic images on **fabrics or wrapping paper** to fill some of the "hours." Use **holiday stamps** and a **black inkpad** to create images on paper for the others. Cut out the paper or fabric motifs, leaving a margin to go behind the clock face, and attach them with **double-stick tape.** Put the clock back together and hang it on your wall.

DIABOLICAL DESK

Put yourself in a scarily studious mood by decking your desk for the season. If you don't have a funky table to paint orange, throw an **orange cloth** over your desk; if your chair isn't black, pin some **black fabric** tightly over it. To make the wall art, buy a **large blank canvas** at an art supply store and choose a bold black and white **graphic print fabric** at your local fabric store. Attach the fabric to the canvas frame with a **staple gun,** stretching it taut and working first on one edge, then the opposite edge, then the two remaining ones. To complete the effect, arrange some black and white accessories on the table and affix some **googly eyes** to the chair with **self-adhesive Velcro dots.**

in stitches

Use glue, tape, and fusible webbing to patch together unique Halloween decorations.

Black and white are the colors of a haunted night when the moon suddenly highlights lurking spooks and wonders. Our fabric crafts add a sophisticated touch when the witching hour is nigh, yet with moon and bird motifs, they're not scary—you can enjoy them throughout the fall and winter seasons. The many no-sew projects are easy to create, and the one enchanting sewn project is sure to cast a spell over any avid quilter who gazes upon it.

moonlight lanterns

Let little crescent moons shed a sliver of light on dark holiday evenings.

For each lantern:
1   candleholder with a cylindrical glass chimney
    (ours is 11 inches tall and 5½ inches in diameter)
1   piece (12 × 18 inches) vellum
1   piece (12 × 18 inches) black construction paper
1   piece of fabric about 1 inch shorter and half as
    wide as the vellum for the "frame" opening (ours
    is about 7 × 10 inches)

1   slightly smaller piece of fabric for the moon
    (in a different print than the frame; ours is about
    4 × 6 inches)
White pencil or chalk

1. Cut the vellum and black construction paper to measure 11 × 18 inches (or the same height as your candleholder and ½ inch longer than its circumference). On the construction paper, use the white pencil to draw a skewed "square" for the outside of the frame opening as shown in the photo, leaving about 1 inch above and below the frame. Draw a smaller skewed square inside that is parallel to the first. Draw a crescent moon inside this square. Use a craft knife to cut out the frame window and the moon.

2. Place the square with the moon cutout face down on your work surface. Put double-stick tape along the outside edges and also along the moon opening (cut small pieces of tape to fit along the curve). Put the moon fabric face down over this and press into place with your hand. Turn the piece over and cut off any excess fabric.

3. Place the large piece of black paper face down on your work surface. Put double-stick tape along the edges of the window opening. Lay the frame fabric face up; place the paper tape-side down on top and press them together. Turn the moon unit wrong side up and put double-stick tape along the edges. Place it tape-side down on the fabric-filled opening in the larger piece of paper and smooth them together.

4. Turn the black paper and fabric unit face down. Affix the vellum to it with double-stick tape placed at intervals along the edges. Wrap the lantern cover around the candleholder tape the overlapped edges closed.

moonlight bird PILLOWS

Iron-on appliqués cut from **fabric scraps** add an elegant finish to **plain pillow covers,** and are quick and easy to make. Ours are just fused in place, but you can enhance yours with embroidery if you like.

Follow the manufacturer's directions to adhere **paper-backed fusible webbing** to the back of your fabric. Copy or scan and print the bird and moon templates on pages 126, enlarging as desired, and cut out (or create your own). Trace onto the paper backing (the image will be reversed when the fabric is face up) and cut it out. Cut out about 12 dots ranging from ½ to ¾ inches in diameter from the scrap fabric.

Peel the paper from the shapes and pin them into place on the pillow cover; iron to fuse them to the cover. Wait 30 minutes before putting the cover back on the pillow.

FASHIONISTA TREAT BAG

This chic little envelope is just the thing to hold a few necessities or tickets to a horror flick—and you can make it in minutes. Cut a 4½ × 14-inch strip of **fabric** with **pinking shears or a rotary cutter** with a decorative blade to cut the fabric. Place the fabric strip wrong side up on your ironing board. Fold over 5 inches at one end and crease the fold with the iron. Slide two 5-inch strips of ½-inch fusible webbing between the layers along the edges; iron according to the web directions. Fold the open end of the bag over 3 inches; crease the fold with the iron. Sew a **button** to the flap or cut a buttonhole in the flap and sew a button to the front of the pouch.

PUMPKIN PATCHED

Here's one project where a **fake pumpkin** works better than a real one. Paint a pumpkin made of foam, papier mâché, or cement (available at craft and garden stores), with **flat black spray paint.** Trace the templates on page 127 (or draw your own) and cut them out. Test the size against your pumpkin (ours is about 10 inches in diameter) and adjust it if you like. Cut the features from **fabric scraps** (the eyes don't have to be symmetrical, just be sure to cut a pair). Referring to the photo, affix the pieces to the pumpkin with **decoupage medium** (such as Mod Podge®), following the manufacturer's directions.

crooked moon quilt

Make a magical 58 × 76-inch quilt for a wall, sofa, or bed. Use the photo as inspiration for the sewed square borders.

5½ yards 45-inch-wide black fabric borders and moon squares

4½ yards 45-inch-wide muslin for the quilt back

4 yards 48-inch-wide muslin for the center panel and moon squares

Fabric marker or chalk, both white and black
Off-white thread
Black thread
Ruler and straightedge

1. From the 48-inch-wide muslin, cut a center panel that measures 47 × 65 inches. Using the remainder of the muslin, cut 22 strips each 2 inches wide. Cut 20 crescent moons, each approximately 8 inches long and 2½ inches wide at the center.

2. Marking across the black fabric, cut twenty 10-inch squares. Then, parallel to the selvage of the remaining black fabric, cut two strips 7 inches wide × 126 inches long. Cut each into 2 pieces, one 65 inches long and one 61 inches long. Set aside all 4 pieces for the borders. Cutting across the remaining black fabric, cut 40 strips each 3½ inches wide.

3. Using the iron, press under about ¼ inch all around each muslin moon shape. Clip the inside curve if you need to. Press under more to vary the finished size if you like.

4. Lay a moon in the middle of each black square; slipstitch in place. Draw a skewed square around each, about 2 inches from the cut edge, marking the shape for the black background. Draw a second line ¼ inch closer to the edge of the square. Cut the square along the outer lines.

5. Lay the square right side up. Align a muslin strip along one edge. Pin the strip in place and cut off the excess. Machine-sew the strip to the square, stitching ¼ inch from the cut edge. Fold the sewn strip over along the seam and press it flat, away from the square. Repeat on each remaining edge of the square. You can sew the second border to the opposite edge or the adjacent edge—we did some each way.

6. Lay a bordered square right side up. Draw a second skewed square outline on the muslin strips.

Draw a second square ¼ inch outside the first and cut the muslin on the outside lines.

7. Repeat step 5 with the 3½-inch-wide black strips. Fold one strip under to create a narrow border on one edge of the square (our borders range from ⅜ to ¾ inch) and press the fold. Repeat with the remaining edges of the square.

8. With the right sides together and the cut edges aligned, pin and then sew a 65-inch black border strip to 1 side edge of the center panel, stitching ½ inch from the edge. Press the seam allowances and border away from the panel. Repeat at the opposite side edge of the panel. Sew the 61-inch black borders to the top and bottom edges of the panel.

9. Cut the backing fabric in half crosswise. Sew the pieces together along 1 long edge, stitching ½ inch from the edge. Press the seam allowances open. Lay the backing right side up on a large flat surface. Center the quilt top right side down on top of it. Pin together along the quilt-top edges. Make sure the layers are smooth and cut off excess backing fabric. Sew the top to the back ½ inch from the edge, leaving an opening on the bottom for turning. Trim the corners and turn the quilt right side out. Press the seam and topstitch ½ inch from the edge all the way around.

10. Lay the center panel right side up. Arrange the moon squares in 5 rows of 4 squares on top; rotate and arrange the squares until you like the overall composition. Pin each square in place, then sew them by hand or machine, stitching along the seam between the outside black strips and the muslin strips.

THe storage Patch

Put your storage unit in a holiday mood by painting it orange and facing the doors with black-and-white fabric. This technique will work for any cabinet with doors; just follow the directions below, using as much paint and fabric as necessary for the size of your furniture.

For the storage unit or cabinet, you will need:
Latex primer paint
Latex semigloss orange paint

For each door, you'll need:
1   square black foam board the same size as the door (ask your art-supply store to cut the foam board to size for you)
1   square fabric 1½ inches larger than the door.

Paintbrushes
Indoor carpet tape
Fabric glue
Hot glue

1. Remove the doors from the storage unit. Remove all the hardware, including the handles; set aside the doors and hardware. Paint the storage unit with 1 coat of primer and 2 coats of orange paint, allowing to dry thoroughly between coats.

2. Measure the location of the doorknob and mark it on each piece of foam board. Pierce where marked using an awl.

3. Place 1 fabric square face down on your ironing board. Fold up a ¾-inch margin along one edge and crease the fold with the iron. Repeat on the opposite edge, and then the remaining edges. Use a dot of fabric glue to secure the folds at the corners. Repeat with each remaining fabric square.

4. Affix a length of tape along each edge of one foam board panel, cutting the tape to fit and removing the protective paper layer from each strip as you go. Invert a prepared fabric square on top, aligning the edges, and press smoothly into place with your hands. Repeat to cover each remaining panel.

5. Turn each panel fabric-side down. One panel at a time, apply hot glue along the edges and in a zigzag pattern over the center; invert panel onto a door and tightly hold the edges together for 1 minute until the glue dries. On each panel, poke the handle hole through the fabric with the awl and then reinstall the handle. Reattach the hinges and rehang the doors on the storage unit.

quickie framed wall quilt

A picture frame with cutouts provides a stained-glass effect for this quick wall hanging. If you prefer, use a regular square frame and skip the directions for the side windows in steps 1 through 3.

1   picture frame (for an 11 × 14-inch picture; the outside measures 16 × 20 inches)
1   sheet (24 × 36 inches) poster board
1   sheet (24 × 36 inches) foam board
Scraps of fabric in different patterns (for the side windows and the center motif; as many as you like)

¾   yard patterned fabric (for large window background)
1   yard of paper-backed fusible webbing
Chalk fabric marker
Double-stick carpet tape

1. Remove the back of the frame and set it aside. Measure and cut one piece of poster board and one piece of foam board to fit inside each of the smaller frame windows (measure from the back to be sure the boards sit against the lip inside the molding).

2. Lay the fabrics for the smaller windows face down and use the poster board pieces as templates to measure the fabric pieces; leave at least 2 inches between the poster board pieces when you lay them on the fabric. Measure and mark a 1-inch margin around each shape for an allowance to wrap to the back of the foam board. Cut them out along the outer lines.

3. Lay each piece of poster board face down and place double-stick tape along its edges, removing the protective paper as you go. Lay the fabric pieces face down. Center each poster board piece tape-side up on the corresponding piece of fabric and wrap the fabric over the edges, pressing onto the tape. Fold the corners neatly and press flat with your fingers. Place a strip of double-stick tape along the middle of each piece, then affix the corresponding piece of foam board to each one.

4. Cover the frame back with the large piece of fabric, affixing the fabric to the edges with double-stick tape and folding the corners neatly. Place the frame over the fabric-covered back and use chalk to mark the outline of the center window onto the fabric. Remove the frame. Draw a chalk line horizontally across fabric in the middle of the marked window opening (use a ruler to measure if you are not comfortable eyeballing it).

5. For the center motif, cut a square of fusible webbing in each of the following sizes: 10 inches, 8 inches, 5 inches, and 4 inches; also cut a 3-inch circle. Follow the manufacturer's directions to fuse each square to the back of a piece of fabric; then cut the fabric along the edge of the paper-backed webbing. Place the fabric-covered frame back face up. Peel the paper backing off the largest square and center it diagonally with the corners on the marked horizontal line; fuse in place. Repeat with the remaining squares and the circle as shown.

6. Place the small fabric-covered pieces into the appropriate frame windows. Place the center piece in the large window. Assemble the frame for hanging.

patterns and basic recipes

These and all of the other patterns and templates used to create the projects in this book can be downloaded from matthewmeadstyle.com. We have also included a couple of recipes that we're sure will become Halloween favorites. Happy crafting!

decoraTInG ICInG

We prefer to use powdered egg whites, such as Just Whites®, for icing recipes like this one in which the egg whites are not cooked. Use this icing for our Masked Scholars (page 36), Screamwiches (page 43), and Hoot Cookies (page 51).

1   box (1 pound) confectioner's sugar
4   teaspoons powdered egg whites (not reconstituted)
⅓   cup water
1   tablespoon fresh lemon juice
1   teaspoon vanilla extract

In a large bowl, beat together all ingredients with an electric mixer at medium speed until just combined, about 1 minute. Increase speed to high and beat icing, scraping down side of bowl occasionally, until it holds stiff peaks, 3 to 5 minutes. Use immediately or cover surface directly with plastic wrap and refrigerate up to 2 days.

Makes about 3 cups

easY ICInG

This icing will become a standby in your recipe repertoire—it's a pure shade of white, so responds well to food color. We use it on our Owl Cake (page 52).

½   cup vegetable shortening
1   teaspoon vanilla extract
½   teaspoon almond extract
½   teaspoon butter flavoring
½   teaspoon salt
4   cups confectioner's sugar

Beat the shortening, vanilla and almond extracts, butter flavoring, and salt in a large mixing bowl with an electric mixer on medium speed for 30 seconds. Slowly add 2 cups confectioner's sugar, beating well. Beat in 2 tablespoons water. Slowly add the remaining 2 cups confectioner's sugar; add 1 to 3 tablespoons more water, as needed, beating to a spreadable consistency.

Makes 4 cups

SPIRIT RAISERS
page 17

BLACK CAT COOKIES
page 37

Enlarge to 125% to make 4-inch-tall cats.

BATTY BOMBE

page 44

For the larger bat wings, follow the orange line; for the smaller wings, use the black template only. Enlarge or shrink as desired.

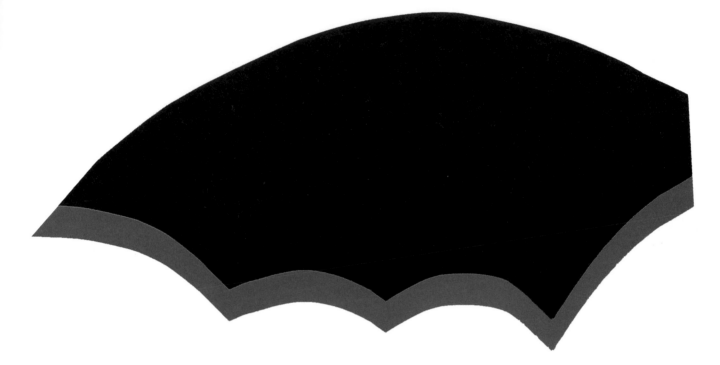

TOOTHY GRIN PLATE

page 57

Enlarge or shrink as needed to fit your plates.

GLITTER JACK BASKETS
page 73

Enlarge or shrink these faces as needed to fit your baskets.

GHOST Garland
page 86

Enlarge to 150% to make 7½-inch ghosts.

candy corn PINCUSHION
page 87

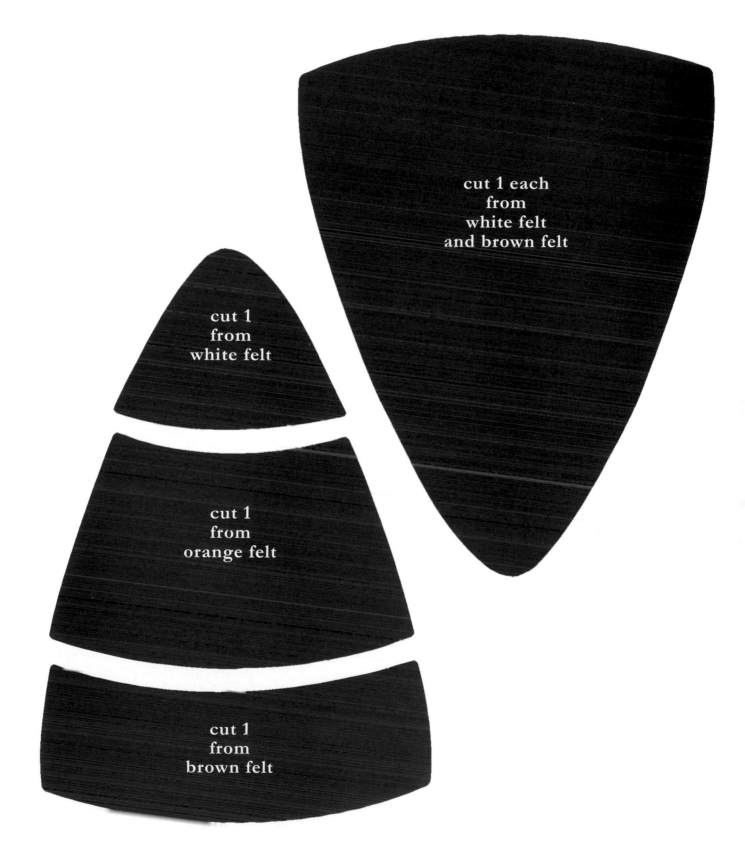

cut 1 each
from
white felt
and brown felt

cut 1
from
white felt

cut 1
from
orange felt

cut 1
from
brown felt

mummy lanterns
page 93

Enlarge or shrink as necessary to fit your lanterns.
Remember to make pairs!

EGGS in DISGUISE
page 97

Brim

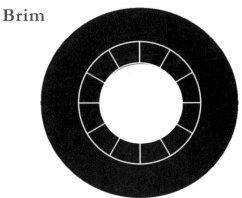

snip tabs and
fold to attach
brim to crown

Crown

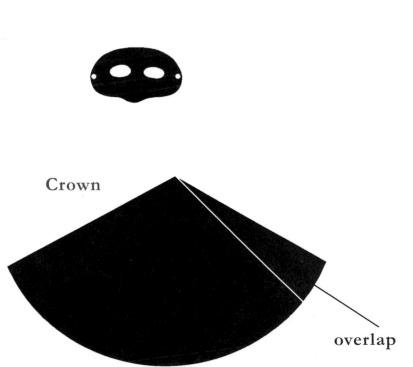

overlap

WALL EYES
page 100

Enlarge or shrink as necessary to fit your plates.

MOONLIGHT BIRD PILLOW
page 108

Enlarge or shrink as needed to fit your pillow.

PUMPKIN PATCHED
page 109

Enlarge or shrink as needed to fit your pumpkin.

project index